Bikes for Rent!

by **Isaac Olaleye**

illustrated by
Chris Demarest

ORCHARD BOOKS • NEW YORK
An Imprint of Scholastic Inc.

For Lisa Atkinson,
who is always cheerful and
always helpful!
— *I.O.*

For Sarah,
my partner on and off the bikes
— *C.D.*

Orchard Books, an imprint of Scholastic Inc.
95 Madison Avenue, New York, NY 10016

Manufactured in the United States of America.
Printed and bound by Phoenix Color Corp.
Book design by Nancy Goldenberg. The text of this book is set in
15.5 point Optima bold The illustrations are watercolor.
10 9 8 7 6 5 4 3 2 1

Library of Congress Cataloging-in-Publication Data
Olaleye, Isaac.
Bikes for rent! / Isaac Olaleye ; illustrated by Chris Demarest.
  p. cm.
Summary: Lateef, a poor young boy living in a village in western Nigeria,
works hard so he can rent a bicycle and ride with the other boys.
ISBN 0-531-30290-3 (trade : alk. paper)
[1. Bicycles and bicycling—Fiction. 2. Nigeria—Fiction.]
I. Demarest, Chris L., ill. II. Title.
PZ7.O423 Bh 2001   [E]—dc21   99-58403

Lateef lived in a village called Erin in the rain forest of western Nigeria. In the middle of the finger-shaped village stood a bicycle stall roofed with palm leaves.

And under that roof worked a stocky man with bushy eyebrows. Babatunde was his name. He rented out old bikes to the village boys. Lateef walked by Babatunde's stall every afternoon after school. "I wish I could rent a bike," Lateef would sigh as he went past. But Lateef's parents were too poor to give him rent money.

Now, Lateef was a determined and hardworking lad. He decided he would earn some rent money. So, day by day, he collected firewood and mushrooms in the rain forest. He sold them in the village market and saved his money in a clay pot.

At last Lateef had enough money. He raced to the bike stall to rent a small blue bike.

Lateef practiced riding. He zigged. He zagged. He fell over and over again. But in a few days, he mastered the small bike. "Yea!" Lateef shouted in delight.

One day when Lateef came to the stall to rent, he couldn't believe his eyes. "Ooh, Babatunde!" he said in wonder.

Babatunde had bought one new, big red bike with a high and straight seat.

"Today I want to rent a *big* one," Lateef said.

But Babatunde rolled out a big, rusty, dented, squeaking bike for Lateef.

Lateef's toes barely touched the pedals. So he leaned right. He leaned left. He zigged. He zagged. He fell.

He practiced and practiced and practiced. He wanted to ride the new red bike!

Soon he mastered the big bike and could ride with no hands. He was now ready for bigger fun.

"Yea!" Lateef shouted.

At the tip of the finger-shaped village was a steep path riddled with potholes. There, up on the hill, the village boys gathered to do tricks on their bikes and to challenge one another.

One day Lateef headed down the sloping path on the big bike.
He looked down the hill. His heart hammered. He stopped!

His friends teased him. "You will never be a good rider. Yea!"
they crowed.

His friends laughed, "Ha-ha, ho-ho, ha-ho!"

The next day, Lateef tried hard to be brave.
He did tricks over one pothole after another.
"Yea!" he shouted.

A few days later, Lateef said, "Babatunde, may I rent your new red bike, please?"

Babatunde said, "No, my boy. Not yet."

As Lateef rode the big, old bike, *fru-fru-fru,* he sang, "I want to ride the new bike, the new red bike. . . . I want to ride it on the mountaintop!"

Each time Lateef rode, Babatunde checked the bike thoroughly.

A few more weeks passed. Lateef asked again to rent the red bike. Babatunde scratched his head. Then he warned Lateef, "Be very, very careful with this bike!"

"I will. I promise," said Lateef.

Lateef whooshed past his friends on the shiny red bike,
spokes flashing silver in the sunlight, and waved. The rubber
horn blared—*beep, beep, beep!*
"Yea," Lateef shouted to his friends.
And they all headed for the hill with their bikes.

One of Lateef's friends challenged him.
"I bet you can't let both hands off the handlebars."

"Easy on this bike," Lateef bragged.

And, hands off the handlebars, he went whooping
down the hill.

Bump! Thump! Whomp!

The bike's wheels spun faster and faster and flew
over pothole after pothole.

Whomp! Wham! Slam bang!

Lateef panicked. He grabbed the handlebars
and pulled hard on both brakes.

Lateef and the bike were now tangled in the sticky
leaves of an aalii shrub.
His friends doubled over with laughter as they
scrambled down the hill.

Lateef slowly pushed the bike to the stall. The front wheel made a strange noise—*kurod, kurod, hug-rod, hug-rod.*

Babatunde exclaimed, "Oh, no! Oh, no! You wrecked my only new bike! You will have to pay five shillings for repairs."

"I will pay you a little every week, Babatunde. I promise!" Lateef said.

So, by selling firewood and mushrooms, Lateef paid Babatunde a little every week. But five shillings would take many weeks to pay off.

One day as he stared enviously at the boys who came to rent, Lateef said, "Babatunde, can I work for you to pay off my debts?"

"I will try you," Babatunde said.

Soon, with Babatunde's teaching, Lateef learned how to fix a bike.
Lateef and Babatunde traveled in a mammy wagon to a big town called Ilesha.
There they bought old bikes and old parts.

Back in the village of Erin, Lateef and Babatunde
built old bikes with old parts.
Finally Lateef had paid all he owed Babatunde.
He no longer had to work at the stall.

But Lateef said, "Babatunde, can I keep my job in exchange for a bike?"

"I am sure we can work something out," Babatunde said with a smile.

"Yea, yea!" Lateef sang as he skipped home.

So, piece by piece, Lateef earned his bike—his very own, almost-new bike.

Lateef showed his friends his lemon yellow, almost-new bike.

"Yea! Yea! Yea!" he shouted with great delight.